Tabu

Mien Potgieter

To order additional copies of this book, contact:
Xlibris
1-800-455-039
www.xlibris.com.au
Orders@Xlibris.com.au

ISBN: Softcover   978-1-7960-0774-9
        EBook   978-1-7960-0773-2

Print information available on the last page

Rev. date: 11/07/2019

Chapter 1

Tabu's Family

The Siamese cat mother looks proudly at her four kittens: Tabu, Tilly, Levi, and Hope. They are all so precious. A tear wells up as she thinks how quickly they have grown up. They are now ready to move onto homes of their own.

Hope is a lady, just like their mother, and Levi enjoys exploring new things. Tabu is peaceful and the dreamer, somewhat unsure of himself. Tilly is an adventurer who is scared of nothing and has a love for listening to the conversations of others. Tabu and Tilly might have opposite personalities, but they almost look identical. They share a very close and loving relationship.

One day, Tilly runs so fast down the corridor that she loses her footing and slides across the floor on her back. She finally comes to a stop against Tabu, who is laughing so hard he has tears rolling down his face.

"What do you think you are laughing at?" asks Tilly with a frown and a piercing look.

"You looked so funny sliding on your back with all four your paws in the air. Why are you in such a rush anyway? Have you done something you shouldn't have, again?" asks Tabu as he squints his eyes.

"Nope, I just couldn't get to you quickly enough to share the good news!" replies Tilly.

"What good news?" asks Tabu with a frown on his face.

"Not until you apologise for laughing at me. You know it's not nice to laugh at someone when they fall. What if I got hurt, would you still be laughing?" Tilly is so upset she wants to keep the news to herself, but she can't bear not sharing it with Tabu.

"Of course not, but you looked pretty funny! I'm sorry."

Tabu barely finishes his sentence when the words start flowing from Tilly's mouth. She shares with him that she heard the people of the house saying that the kittens are now big enough to go to homes of their own.

"What does that mean?" asks Tabu with an even bigger frown than before.

"It means that people who love cats will take us to their homes, where we will live for ever and ever. We will have a home of our own somewhere in the world. It's so exciting!" exclaims Tilly.

"I don't want to go anywhere!" says Tabu as he turns his back to Tilly.

"Why not? I can't wait to explore the world and have a home of my own. Just think of all the new places you will get to see," says Tilly with renewed excitement glimmering in her eyes.

"I'm not so sure," says Tabu as he looks back at Tilly over his shoulder. Thoughts of never seeing Tilly or the rest of his family brings tears to his eyes, but he looks away before Tilly can see. Then a thought crosses his mind. It could be very exciting to see the world.

Tilly says that they might need to go on an airplane. She once saw the people pointing at a big iron bird flying through the clouds in the sky, calling it an airplane. She silently wishes that she could go on an airplane and wonders what she would see from up there.

"I'm going back to see if I can find out more about where we are going." The last bit of the sentence disappears with Tilly as she rushes around the corner.

Tabu lies down on the sunny pillow in front of the window. He wonders what it would be like to go outside. Tilly says that they are not allowed to go outside because they can get very sick. She says that it is very dangerous and that it is better to listen now than to be sorry later. The thoughts play through his head as the warmth of the sun makes him drift off to sleep.

The next minute, Tabu wakes up with Tilly on top of him, pulling at his ears. "Wake up! Wake up!" she shouts excitedly. He jumps up confused and in a daze. "What's wrong? Why are you shouting?"

Tilly is dancing round and round, and it looks like she is trying to catch her tail. "I'm going to Rakaia!" she shouts with excitement. "There is absolutely no way to get there with a car, so I'm going to go on the big iron bird. I can't wait. Rakaia is on the South Island of New Zealand." She finally finishes out of breath.

"Where am I going?" asks Tabu with a fear-filled voice.

"I don't know," answers Tilly. "I'm just so excited and can't wait for tomorrow."

"Tomorrow!" says Tabu with hesitation as he looks at her with surprise in his eyes.

"Yes, tomorrow. Isn't it exciting? Before the sun rises tomorrow, I will be gone."

Tabu looks at his sister, and a tear rolls down his furry cheek. Then another, and another.

"Don't cry, Tabu. Be happy for me." She gives him a big hug.

The next morning, Tabu wakes up without Tilly in the house. He wanders around in the house, sad and restless. It's just not the same without his bubbly sister who has now been given a home of her own. He wonders if he will ever see her again.

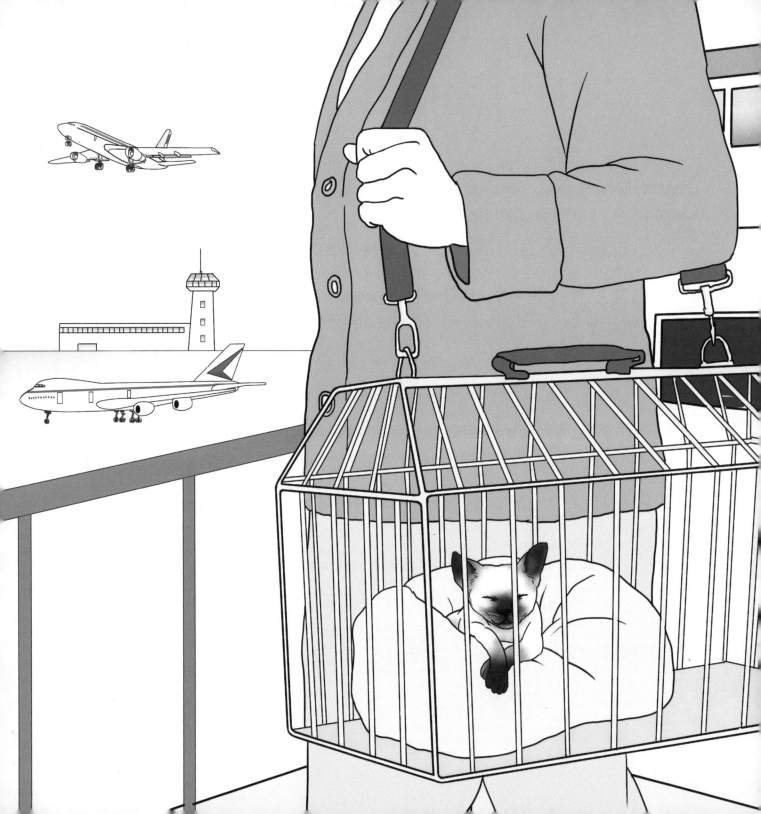

Chapter 2

Tabu's New Home

One sunny morning, Tabu wakes up to the news that it is his turn to go to a new home. He is loaded into a special small, cosy, travelling box and placed into the car. Tabu is sad, but at the same time excited. Things are just not the same without his beloved sister, Tilly. He doesn't know where he is going, but he is looking forward to having a human family of his own. Maybe he won't miss Tilly as much when he has a home of his own.

The car comes to a stop, and when they take him out, he sees all the iron birds that Tilly used to talk about. Suddenly he feels a bit scared at the thought that he is going to fly in one of those noisy iron birds.

They walk into a building, where it becomes quieter. The humans take him out of the box and stroke him gently. They talk softly while giving him a tablet that the humans say will help him to sleep. It doesn't take long before he starts to get sleepy. He tries to keep his eyes open to see where they are taking him, but the movement makes him drift off into a deep sleep.

A gentle stroke from his head to his toes, with a soft voice, wakes him. He tries to open his eyes, but he still feels tired. He wonders why they give him a tablet to help him sleep and now they want to wake him again.

Tabu does not recognise the soft voice and wants to see who is stroking him so gently. He forces his eyes open and sees an elderly man and woman. The old man speaks, and Tabu recognises it as the soft voice that woke him. "This is your new home, and we are your new owners," he says with a smile. "My name is Joe, and this is my wife, Anne."

Tabu looks around. He is no longer in the box but is lying on top of a big pillow in front of a warm, glowing fire. The man slowly reaches out to Tabu and picks him up, ever so gently, and places him on his lap. Tabu feels spoiled and loved. "So this is my new home and my new family. I wonder where in the world I am. I think I'm going to be happy here, wherever this is." He will never forget Tilly, but being in this loving home will make the longing better.

Tabu has his own bed, special blanket, and lots of new toys. That night, he sleeps like a rock.

For the next three days, Tabuis not allowed to go outside. He jumps onto the couch and then onto the windowsill to see what it looks like outside. The garden is beautiful and filled with lots of colourful flowers. There is a big green lawn and Tabu can't wait to roll on it and play outside.

He jumps off and continues to explore the house, room by room. He struggles to jump onto the bed, but his sharp nails help him to hold on tightly. Finally, he reaches the top and sees an unfamiliar object on the table next to the bed. He walks over to look and has a massive fright when he sees another cat opposite him. *I didn't know there was another cat in this house,* he thinks.

Slowly Tabu moves forward to have a closer look. The other cat also moves forward slowly. Tabu stops, and the other cat also stops. When Tabu moves, the other cat also moves. *Is this Tilly trying to play another trick on him?* Tabu gets so excited about the idea of being with his beloved sister again that he gathers all his courage and moves forward to smell Tilly. He puts his nose against her nose. It is cold and doesn't smell like anything. He tries to touch Tilly, but it just feels cold. He tries to put his paw behind the cold barrier between them, but there is nothing there. When he looks at the front, he sees her looking back at him, but when he looks at the back, there is nothing. *How am I going to get her out of here?* he wonders.

He starts to meow as loudly as he can. Just then, he sees the friendly smile of Anne behind Tilly. "Tabu, have you never seen a mirror before?" she asks in a friendly voice. "You are seeing your own reflection in the mirror." She picks him up and gives him a gentle hug.

Tabu feels sad as he realises that he was looking at himself and not Tilly. He is surprised by how much he misses her. He jumps back onto the couch and then the windowsill. Anne notices that Tabu is sad and points to a small, colourful flying thing outside. "That is a butterfly, Tabu," she says as the butterfly lands on a flower.

Tabu looks at the butterfly, mesmerised by its beauty. He wonders what that is and can't wait to play with it once he is allowed outside. *Looks like I still have a lot to learn about the world,* he thinks. Suddenly he gets very excited about the idea of discovering more of what is out there. Maybe that will help him not miss Tilly so much.

The windowsill looking out into the garden and road has become Tabu's favourite spot. In the afternoons, he watches the children playing with the ball and wants to play with them. Anne also has a ball, but she doesn't play with it. She has two sticks that go click-clack as they move across each other to make a blanket just like the one on his bed. He really wants to play with the ball and hits it with his paw. It flies over the floor, and he chases after it.

"No, Tabu, that's not a ball. It's my knitting wool," Anne says.

She fetches another ball for Tabu from his toys. Tabu enjoys playing with the ball. He lies on his back and kicks the ball up into the air with all four paws. Then he chases it across the room. It rolls under a cupboard, and Tabu lies flat on his stomach to try reaching the ball. Sometimes he can get it on his own, but other times, Anne has to help. She uses a stick with lots of feathers on one end. He tries to help, but she says it's best to wait as they can't both try at the same time. Each day, Tabu discovers something new and exciting. Tabu loves all his toys, but when he is tired, he lies on Anne's lap for a nap. He loves lying around her neck with his feet hanging down like a scarf or sitting on her shoulder.

Chapter 3

Tabu's First Day Outside

At last, the three days are over and Tabu is very excited to explore outside. Joe gently carries Tabu outside to the middle of the lawn. He sits down with Tabu on his lap then gives him a nudge "Off you go."

Unsure, Tabu puts one paw on the grass, then the next, and finally he has all four paws on the grass. It is cold and tickles him a bit. He likes the soft, cool feeling under his paws. He starts running in a circle around Joe and then jumps back onto Joe's lap. Joe laughs loudly.

Joe plays with him for a bit and then says that he needs to go back inside but that Tabu can keep playing outside.

Tabu likes being outside in the garden. He sniffs here, looks there, and explores a bit more. He smells the flowers and chases the butterflies. He finally sits quietly for a minute to look at all the other houses around him.

Suddenly something jumps on top of him from behind. He jumps up into the air, feeling his hair stand up on his back. He lands on his feet and thinks he is dreaming. He can't believe what he is seeing.

Is this a reflection in a mirror, or can it really be? The laughter sounds exactly like Tilly.

"I gave you a good old fright, didn't I?" says Tilly.

Tabu cannot believe his eyes. It truly is Tilly! He is so excited that he grabs her around the waist and starts to dance on the grass.

"How did you know I was here?" he asks with a puzzled look.

"Just kind of overheard it," she says casually.

"Don't lie! You were listening to the humans' conversations again, weren't you?"

"Yes, OK, I was, but aren't you glad? Otherwise, I would not have known that you were here."

Tilly starts to tell Tabu how she came looking for him every day and how glad she was when he finally came into the garden today. She had to hide in between the flowers to make sure that it was indeed Tabu before she jumped on top of him.

"I heard that your old man has depression, which means that he never laughs and is always sad. I also heard that a cat or dog is the best medicine to treat it," says Tilly with confidence. "It must be true, because I saw him laughing while he was playing with you on the grass today. I'm sure he will get better very soon."

"Come. I want to show you something," says Tilly as she drags Tabu around the corner of the house. "That big, white house on the other side of the fence is where I live, and this is the hole in the fence where I crept through to come visit you!"

She continues. "My human family is very kind and has two little girls. During the day, they go to school, and in the afternoon, they carry me around and brush my fur. In the evenings, I sleep with one of them in their warm bed. The one is called Tina, and the other is called Tammy, and they are twins," says Tilly. "Look. There they are now."

Tabu looks as two blonde girls cross the road and walk in their direction.

"Bye-bye, Tabu. I'll see you again tomorrow."

Tabu still wants to say something, but Tilly slips back through the hole in the fence. Tabu can hear the girls calling Tilly.

Tabu blinks a few times. He still can't believe his eyes. *Is it just a dream?*

"Oh, there you are," says Joe as he picks Tabu up and strokes his head.

Tabu pushes against Joe's chest, enjoying every pampering moment.

"Come. You have not eaten anything all day," says Joe as he slowly walks towards the house.

As they reach the door, Joe puts Tabu down. "Look. This is your own little door so that you can come and go as you please. It's just very important that you always come back."

Joe bends down and shows Tabu how the little flap door works. Tabu looks at the door with suspicion and uncertainty. He then realises that it will give him the freedom to go outside to see Tilly at any time. He gathers all his courage and nudges the door open with his head.

"Now that wasn't so hard, was it?" says Joe as he strokes Tabu. Tabu feels very proud that he did it. He turns around and goes back outside, then back inside and outside and inside. Joe laughs. "That's enough practise for now. You need to come eat something."

Tabu didn't realise how hungry he was from all the play and excitement of the day. After he finishes his meal, he goes to lie on the windowsill, where he falls asleep, dreaming of Tilly and playing with her in the garden.

Tabu is very happy in his new home with his new human family. The longer he lives there, the more he feels like a human. Joe even says that he is their little Siamese child.

In the summer, Tabu slept on the bed at Anne's feet. Now that it is winter, it is very cold and Tabu is allowed to sleep next to Anne. He once nudges his nose under her arm and she lifts it, allowing him to crawl in under the blankets. It is the cosiest, warmest place in the whole, wide world.

Chapter 4

Tabu's First Winter

One winter's morning, Tabu crawls out from under the blankets with a long yawn and big stretch.

It is very cold, so he decides to lie down in his favourite sunny spot on the windowsill. He sees Anne putting pieces of wood in the hole in the wall.

"Tabu," she says with a very serious voice, "this is a fireplace, and it is nice and warm, but you need to be very careful as you can burn yourself if you get too close. I'm going to light the fire now."

Tabu watches as the fire starts to glow in colours of yellow, orange, red, purple, and white.

"Did you see it snowed last night, Tabu?" Anne asks.

Tabu does not know what snow is and jumps onto the windowsill. He almost falls off when he sees that everything outside looks so different.

"Isn't it beautiful? The snow transforms everything into a white, winter wonderland," explains Anne when she notices the confusion on Tabu's face.

So snow is all that white stuff that takes away the colour in the garden, thinks Tabu.

He learns about all the different colours from Tilly, who learned it from the twins. Tilly tells him that they know a lot about the world, and they learn it at school. Tabu is not sure what to think of the snow, but the more he looks at it, the more he likes it. It looks like the trees and the rest of the garden are covered in a white blanket. Maybe the white blanket keeps the garden warm from this cold winter. *Where is the sun? Is it covered in a white blanket too?* He looks at the glowing fire, wondering if it is there to replace the sun.

He looks back at the window and sees small white feathers falling from the sky. He pushes his nose up against the window, but suddenly it becomes so foggy that he can't see anything.

Anne wipes the window and explains that the white flakes falling from the sky are snow.

Tabu is excited to see if the trees at Tilly's house are also covered in a white blanket. He jumps down from the windowsill, jumps through his door to the outside, and lands in the snow. The snow is soft, and Tabu almost disappears completely in the snow. *Brrr, it's cold.*

Tabu tries to walk but realises that it is a bit tricky. He sinks into the snow with each step he takes. After a big struggle, he is finally out of the snow and jumps back into the house. He shakes his paws and licks at the white snow stuck on his fur. *No, thank you. This cold blanket can stay outside*, thinks Tabu as he suddenly starts to feel sorry for all the trees covered in this cold blanket.

Anne places a pillow in front of the fireplace and invites him over. "Here you go, boy. Make yourself comfortable. I think it is going to snow the whole day."

Tabu lies down, and it doesn't take long for the warmth of the fire to dry his body and put him to sleep.

The sound of laughter wakes him. Curiously, he jumps onto the windowsill to investigate where the laughter is coming from. It's not snowing anymore, and the twins are playing in the snow. They are dressed in a lot of clothes, and their hands and heads are covered. They are making something with big, round balls and carrots.

Tabu decides that the next time he goes outside, he will definitely have to wear something warm. Maybe something that Anne has been making with the sticks that go click-clack. A blanket and maybe a sock on his head and feet.

After a few days, the snow melts and now everything is brown and muddy. Tabu ventures back outside to see if he can see Tilly. He waits at the hole in the fence but doesn't see or hear anything. Sad, he turns around when Tilly suddenly jumps on his back. Annoyed, he swings around, but suddenly his anger turns into a smile and then laughter.

"What is so funny?" asks Tilly with a sharpness in her voice.

Tabu looks at his sister, who is dressed in a cardigan and tutu with a bow tied around her ears. As if she knows what he is thinking, Tilly stands on her back legs and does a bit of a dance. She tells him that the twins dress her in their doll clothes. At the beginning, she didn't like it, but now she kind of likes it. Socks on her feet is where she draws the line. She shakes them off every time.

As Tilly makes another twirl in her tutu, Tabu thinks about the past few months. It has been filled with lots of first experiences, including the ride in the iron bird, the white blankets of snow, his wonderful human family, and finally meeting Tilly again.

Tabu starts dreaming about all the crazy adventures that are to come, because with Tillie, anything is possible. And then Tabu realises that he might be an adventurous cat after all. With a sister like Tilly, he has to be.

CPSIA information can be obtained
at www.ICGtesting.com
Printed in the USA
BVHW021215211119
564440BV00002B/6/P